FRANKIE GETS A DOGGIE

AMY HUNTINGTON

BOYDS MILLS PRESS

AN IMPRINT OF BOYDS MILLS & KANE

New York

In memory of my mom—
teacher of kids and lover of dogs.
"Woof, woof."
—AH

For information about permission to reproduce selections
from this book, please contact permissions@bmkbooks.com.

Boyds Mills Press
An imprint of Boyds Mills & Kane, a division of Astra Publishing House
boydsmillspress.com
Printed in China

ISBN: 978-1-63592-320-9 (hc)
ISBN: 978-1-63592-468-8 (eBook)
Library of Congress Control Number: 2020947624

First edition
10 9 8 7 6 5 4 3 2 1

Design by Barbara Grzeslo
The text is set in Neutraface Demi.
The title is hand-lettered by Amy Huntington.
The illustrations are done in gouache and digital media.

. . . gathers up some shoes,
Papa's getting ready,
says it's time to cruise.

Kisses to the kitty,

stroller made for two,
Papa pushes Frankie
down the avenue.

Frankie smiles and wiggles.
"Goodness, how you've grown!
Let's go meet some doggies,
maybe take one home?"

Wagging tails, wet noses,
straight or floppy ears,
fur that's short or shaggy,
lots of doggies here.

Some dogs knock you over,

some dogs shy away . . .

. . . some will yip or yawn. Oh!

This dog wants to play!

Sloppy, soggy kisses,
a proper howdy-do.
Papa whispers softly,
"Ah . . . she sure likes you."

Sweet and snuggly Doggie
lies down for a pet.
Hugs and belly tickles,
Frankie's choice is set!

Sniff,
sniff.

Chip,
chip,
chip!

Brand-new smells and noises,
games of peek-a-boo,

Frankie pushes Doggie
up the avenue.

Doggie greets the kitty.
Kitty fluffs his fur.
He is none too happy!
Takes off in a blur.

Doggie keeps her distance.
Kitty hides away.

Frankie wants these buddies
to get along and play.

Brimming bowls of kibble
lighten up their moods.

Frankie's pets and scratches
improve their attitudes.

Papa reads to Frankie.
Kitty's in the sun.
Doggie's found her family . . .

. . . love for everyone.